Editor: Christianne Jones
Page Production: Tracy Davies
Creative Director: Keith Griffin
Editorial Director: Carol Jones
Managing Editor: Catherine Neitge

First American edition published in 2006 by
Picture Window Books
5115 Excelsior Boulevard
Suite 232
Minneapolis, MN 55416
877-845-8392
www.picturewindowbooks.com

Copyright © 2004 by Allegra Publishing Limited
Unit 13/15 Quayside Lodge
William Morris Way
Townmead Road
London SW6 2UZ UK

The art in this book was colored by Datagraph System.

Printed in the United States of America.

Library of Congress Cataloging-in-Publication Data
Law, Felicia.
Rumble meets Eli Elephant / by Felicia Law ; illustrated by Yoon-Mi Pak.—1st
American ed.
p. cm. — (Read-it! readers)
Summary: Rumble the dragon has hired an orchestra for the grand opening of his
Cave Hotel, but the conductor may not be able to fit through the front door.
ISBN 1-4048-1332-2 (hard cover)
[1. Conductors (Music)—Fiction. 2. Elephants—Fiction. 3. Dragons—Fiction.
4. Caves—Fiction.] I. Pak, Yoon-Mi, ill. II. Title. III. Series.

PZ7.L41835Rume 2005
[E]—dc22   2005007359

Rumble Meets Eli Elephant

by Felicia Law
illustrated by Yoon-Mi Pak

Special thanks to our advisers for their expertise:

Adria F. Klein, Ph.D.
Professor Emeritus, California State University
San Bernardino, California

Susan Kesselring, M.A.
Literacy Educator
Rosemount–Apple Valley–Eagan (Minnesota) School District

PiCTURE WiNDOW BOOKS
Minneapolis, Minnesota

This is a story of a cool, young dragon named Rumble. When his grandma leaves her run-down cave to him, Rumble sets about making it into a four-star hotel. He doesn't do it all alone. He has help from a picky hotel inspector and an annoying spider named Shelby.

Rumble's Cave Hotel is
becoming very grand.
Rumble has even hired an
orchestra to come and play.
But will its conductor be able to
squeeze through the door?

"Mr. Rumble," clucked Milly the maid, "there's a very large elephant stuck in the doorway of the hotel. He isn't able to come in, and he isn't able to go out. He's stuck!"

"An elephant?" asked Rumble. "Oh good! That means the orchestra has arrived. The elephant is the conductor. Are all the musicians stuck or just the conductor?"

"There's no one else here," said Milly. "It's just the elephant. Will you come and help me push?"

"I'll come at once," said Rumble.

"And me," said Chester the chef.

"Me, too," said Shelby Spider.

9

"Up a bit," said Eli Elephant. "Down a bit. Back a bit. Now forward a bit."

What a squeeze! Everyone pushed and pulled, but the elephant didn't move.

"Let's try a little butter," said Chester. "That might work!"

The butter did the trick! Once Eli was
buttery, he slipped through the doorway
and into the reception area.

"Sorry! It happens all the time," said Eli.
"There are very few doors I can get through.
Let me introduce myself. I'm Eli Elephant, the
conductor of the orchestra."

"Let me show you what I can do! I raise my baton, and the music begins. First the violins, then the bass, and then the clarinets. Now hear the trumpets and the drums. I wave my baton faster, and the music gets faster—a la la! I wave my baton higher, and the music gets louder—bim, bam, boom!" yelled Eli.

"Can anyone hear anything," asked Shelby, "or is it just me?"

15

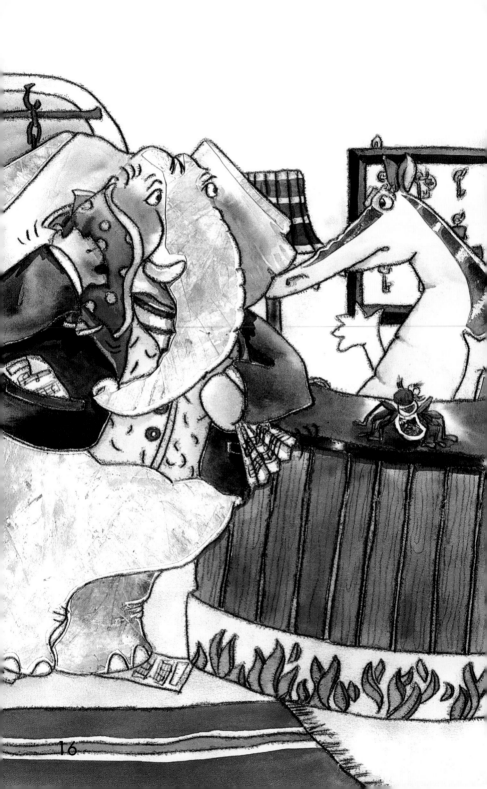

"Excuse me, sir," said Rumble. "I'm sure you're a very good conductor, but where is the orchestra?"

"Ah!" said Eli. "We may have a problem."

Eli explained that he often got stuck in doorways. The members of the orchestra were so used to this that they stayed in the forest until Eli was safely inside. Then, they followed him.

"But the Rumble's Cave Hotel celebration is tomorrow," said Rumble. "We need to practice NOW!"

"A famous singer is coming," grumbled Rumble, blowing an angry puff of smoke. "And my grandma is coming to dance. We MUST have the orchestra."

"I can play," said Shelby.

"Play what?" asked Rumble.

"I can play a musical instrument," said Shelby.

19

Shelby took out her banjo. She plucked, and pinged, and twanged, and finished her act with a tap dance.

Tippety-toe, tippety-tee, tippety-ta ...

"No! No! No!" said Eli.

"No!" said Rumble.

Eli looked around. "Does anyone else play an instrument?" he asked.

But no one did.

20

"I forgot about the practice," said Eli. "But the orchestra will be waiting somewhere in the forest. I'll go and search for it at once."

"I thought elephants never forgot anything," said Shelby. "And another thing, have you forgot that you won't be able to get out of the hotel door?"

But this time, Eli easily slipped through the door. He slid all the way down the valley on his big, buttery backside.

"He'll never find his orchestra in that huge forest," said Rumble sadly.

"Too bad," said Shelby. "He could have had me in his orchestra!"

But Eli did find his orchestra. They were far away, among the tall trees of the forest.

From the hotel, Rumble and Shelby heard a small, tiny toot and a long, low boom.

Then, in the distance, among the shadows of the low branches, they saw a flash of shiny metal and heard the sound of heavy feet.

And, from the hotel entrance, they watched as a line of musicians with musical

instruments of every shape and size
marched up the hillside toward the cave.

"There," said Eli, as he got to the top of the hill. "We have an orchestra! Now, quiet please. We're going to practice."

He waved his baton in the air, and the players took up their instruments. They plucked, and twanged, and screeched, and banged for all they were worth.

WHAT A NOISE! thought Rumble. But at least he would have music for the big Rumble's Cave Hotel celebration.

More *Read-it!* Readers

Bright pictures and fun stories help you practice your reading skills. Look for more books at your level.

Happy Birthday, Gus! by Jacklyn Williams

Happy Easter, Gus! by Jacklyn Williams

Happy Halloween, Gus! by Jacklyn Williams

Happy Thanksgiving, Gus! by Jacklyn Williams

Happy Valentine's Day, Gus! by Jacklyn Williams

Matt Goes to Mars by Carole Tremblay

Merry Christmas, Gus! by Jacklyn Williams

Rumble Meets Buddy Beaver by Felicia Law

Rumble Meets Eli Elephant by Felicia Law

Rumble Meets Keesha Kangaroo by Felicia Law

Rumble Meets Penny Panther by Felicia Law

Rumble Meets Wally Warthog by Felicia Law

Looking for a specific title or level? A complete list of *Read-it!* Readers is available on our Web site:
www.picturewindowbooks.com

32